Roots & Roses

Poems

Cecily Michelle Hillman

CM PUBLISHING

Published by CM Publishing

Misscm.org

This is a work of creative nonfiction. Any references to celebrities or public figures are solely for entertainment purposes.

Cover art: Kozakura Designs

ISBN

979 8 234 05135 6

Dedication

Rebel, every piece of art I create is a reflection of the love I have for you. Thank you for making Mommy's heart smile, and giving me a reason to keep pushing every day. I'll love you forever and ever and ever. To the love of my life: I carry you ***in my heart, eternally. Thank you for keeping me grounded, for lifting me up high, and being my everlasting friend. You inspired the bulk of this work—my biggest muse. I love you!***

Mom, you always taught me to "put God first;" and it's because of the faith you instilled in me that I've survived every storm that has come my way, and gained the insight to write beautiful poetry about it. I love you. Daddy, thank you for forever walking with me, even when I couldn't see your footsteps. I now know you were always by my side, and those moments when I didn't see your strides were the times you covered *me with your heaviest protection. I love you.*

Glennise: ***Your big sister will always love you*** *and be amazed by you.* ***I'm so proud of you!*** *Our journey together has not only strengthened our bond, and us as individuals, but it has been a true testament to what the power of faith can do. I'm deeply inspired by your strength, and your resilience. Thank you for being such a bright light, and* ***my best friend. To my soul tribe worldwide: Words couldn't express the depth of gratitude I have for you all. Thank you for your prayers, your encouragement, and your roots and roses.***

Roots & Roses

Table of Contents

Part II: The Buds ... Page 29

PART I

The Roots

ABSTRACT

Pink

Green

Blue

BEAN

World

SEEN

LOVE

Clean

Big

Small

TRUST

FALL

ROCK

Climb

Slip

Grip

Rise: Come.

Down. To.

Size.

RELATE

Inspire

Mediate

Empire

Mend

Blend

Be — gin

A ✖ gain

Together SOW UBUNTU

Build REAP Kuumba

Laugh GOOD Justice

LIVE Blessings NIA

LEARN FAMILY CREED

EARN HEALTH OHANA

FORGIVE PEACE SAMBA, RWANDA

Genuine JOY BARACK

Authentic UNITY OBAMA

BLUE

Smells like an ocean breeze

Or clean linen dipped in sacred seas

Tastes like fresh berries

Or summertime ice pops topped with cherries

Feels like water, cool and flowing

Or rough, same as denim, stitched from sewing

Makes your eyes sparkle, when you hear and see

Jays blue-ing, humming hymns in a holy tree

Peaceful.

Like the color blue.

To Ty

I loved you the first time my **eyes** met yours

It was like looking in the mirror, and seeing myself

How could I love me, and not love you?

Knowing that you love me because I *am* you?

I see Taki in you

I loved him

I love you

Something deep and internal told me that he and I

would be together

And that feeling was proven true, through you

Eternity is a trip, ain't it?

Like, we're really in this together.

FOREVER.

Changing forms.

Mutating.

Dying.

Living.

Growing.

But NEVER forgetting home.

You.

Me.

Us.

We.

I will one day bear your children

And know what it's like to carry you inside me

And to feel that you are home

Seeds planted in my womb, like how it was before

Like how it all started:

You.

Me.

Us.

We.

Forever. Home.

OUR BACKYARD

I want to keep you, forever
So I gather every memory of your existence
and plant your essence
in my backyard

I can still taste your candy elixir as our
cherry blossoms
Still steal sniffs of your signature scent as stems
seek sun
STILL feel the electricity in your fingertips as petals
promise peacocks
Flower fields forever hear the twist of your tongue as
branches dance
in the day light

You are mine, eternally
Because I cradled you way down

Far enough to keep you safe
Deep enough to drown
So when the "uglies" come lookin' for our
secret treasures
They'll get lost in the language of
our love
And our vaulted Valentine will *never*
be found

How glorious, I get to pick you up and dig you out whenever I
need nourishment
What a privilege to have your memory buried *so deep*
in my backyard
God gave us a gift
So I harvest you with passionate prayer
And consume you with gracious intent

Some days, I just sit
And enjoy our fruits
On the front porch in my rocking chair

Watching our memories run wild

Growing big

Standing tall

Sprouting in *every* corner of our yard

Yes, I know our seeds will surely carry on our sweetness

And take root right here at home

Deep, *deep* down in this here backyard

So I could keep you *forever*

And the existence of YOU

Of ME

Of US

Will *never* be forgotten

Because it's buried *deep* down in our backyard

The *Ruckus*

(ME!)

How dare you be great?

Who told you it was okay to be bold?

The audacity to take hold of your fate

And follow the pathways of your soul

Who do you think you are?

Shining that big, bright light?

Why don't you dim it down a little,

and make me feel alright?

What's the deal with you?

Why you ALWAYS gotta be seen?

You get on my *LAST* nerve,

steady accomplishing all your **dreams**

Why can't it be me?

ME! *ME!*

For once, just me.

NOOOOO! Here YOU come

Takin' up *alllllll* the space with your fancy eagle wings

Why you gotta fly so high?

Can't you come down low?

I tried to bury you with a lie

But all you did was ... grow

THE NERVE!

The arrogance, the conceit, the gall

You dodge EVERY shot that I serve

STOP MAKing me feel so small

I guess I'd better stop

Seems I'm only making you **stronger**

You're getting rougher and tougher

I can't take this much longer

Maybe, just maybe, one day you'll see
That you wouldn't be this unbreakable,
had it not been for *me*
And you'll have a little mercy on me
When you finally reach the top
Knowing I was afraid you'd leave
But never wanting you to stop
And all the while wishing...

That I could dance in your shoes,
That I could one day take your spot

The Rebuttal

(WE!!)

How dare I be great?

Who told me it was okay to be bold?

The **ancestors** who carried the weight

And gave me the language to **communicate**

their countless stories untold

Who are YOU to try to get in my way

And undo what's already been done?

How naïve of you to think that you could sabotage **God's** relay

When the marathon's already been won

Should I sag like old laundry bags?

Feeling filthy with defeat?

Or slump. And stroll in a drag

Beat down, exhausted, and weak?

HA! Not **EYE** boo!

If yo' raggedy a$$ would stop worryin' '

bout what I was doing,

then maybe it *COULD* be YOU!

Are you proud of hanging way down there?

Ain't you got no class?

You lucky that I AM taking the **high** road

Otherwise, I'd tell you to kiss my black a$$!

SICK!

That's what it's called

But I pray you open your heart for the remedy

And get you some **peace** installed

God set these feet on **fire** when she passed me the baton,

'cause I ain't stopped running since

I done lapped yo' loopy behind 2 or 3 times,

by now, ain't you convinced?

And I AM unbreakable, but that ain't because of *yo'* dirt!

I broke through the darkness reaching for the **source**;

this is all GOD'S work!

MERCY?! I'll leave that to your maker

But fi now, sit back and watch me as I pull in this peace,

pick up my **power**, and pack up this paper

Mama's Slumber

I think Mama's in a slumber
Somewhere far, far away

But when she wakes ...

Fear vs. *Love*

What is **fear**?

It is the opposite of **love**

So why should I **fear**

When I've felt the **tenderness** in all that is, what will be,

and everything that was?

I've soaked in centuries of sunsets

Paraded in **paradise**

Been blessed by sunrise

My mouth has sucked in cool water

My body baptized in rivers, holy like my mother's **womb**

I've two-stepped with ghetto sons and daughters

Eyes watched concrete **roses** bloom

My feet fortified by forever **fathers**

And exalted by eternal **brothers**

Spirit fed through the mirror of magical **sisters**

And nourished by the breasts of a million **mothers**

So why should I **fear**?

When my mind had imagined **pretty purples**,

glorious greens, **and billowing blues**

And my heart has **electrified** the frequencies of a

thousand and one, **perpetual hues**

I don't **fear**. I **love**.

Because I know the **sweet**, everlasting **victory** of all that is,

what will be, and everything that was

30 SHADES OF BLACK

MY BLACK IS GREEN
GREEN LIKE PASTELES, FALAFELS, AND GALLO PINTO BEANS
GREEN LIKE PLANTAINS AND CURRIED CHICKEN, STEWED AND STEAMED
OR TOSTONES, HOOKED UP WITH SOME FUNKY CALLALOO, OR SOUTHERN COLLARD GREENS

MY BLACK IS BLUE
BLUE LIKE CONCH FRITTERS, AND FRIED LIONFISH TOO
BLUE LIKE BLUE CORN TORTILLAS AND NASI KERABU
MIAMI BLUE, SAME AS THE BUTTERFLY PEA FLOWER HUE
OR DEEPER AND DARKER,
LIKE HAITIAN-STYLE BLUE FISH
AND LA BANDERA DOMINICANA,
SUMMERTIME, ON A HOT HARLEM STOOP

MY BLACK IS RED
RED LIKE KOOL-AID, WITH A WHOLE LOTTA SUGAR

BRIGHT RED LIKE MASALA
OR "GOOD NIGHT" RED, LIKE THAT ITIS
ESCOVITCH THAT YOU EAT WITH ONE FOOT UP
RED THAT'LL MAKE YOUR EARS STEAM, LIKE
PEPPERED MATOKE OR DORO WAT
HOT! RED HOT, THAT'LL MAKE YOUR NOSE BLEED, LIKE HARISSA, COOKED SLOW WITH KEFTA, IN A TAGINE POT

CHIIIIIIIIIILLLLLLEEEE! I'M ***YELLOW*** BLACK LIKE CORNBREAD, CHITTERLINGS, AND TEXAS FRIED CHICKEN, THAT YOU HIT WITH A DAB OF MUSTARD
YELLOW LIKE MAC AND CHEESE, PEACH COBBLER, OR NANA'S 'NANA PUDDING, PUMPED UP WITH EXTRA CUSTARD
HIGH YELLA, LIKE EGG FOO YOUNG, EMPANADAS, ROTI, MOFONGO AND ARROZ AMARILLO
I'M TALKIN' YELLOW BONE YELLOW, CHOMPING ON ABUELO'S TAMALES DE TICHINDA, OR YUCA CON MOJO

ORANGE-BLACK, LIKE CANDIED YAMS AND SWEET POTATO PIE, THAT SENDS "BROTHERLY LOVE" STRAIGHT TO YOUR HEART
OR A BIG BOWL OF JOLLOF THAT YOU INHALE ON AN EARLY AUTUMN STROLL THROUGH BRANCH BROOK PARK

FEIJOADA WITH A SLICE OF ORANGE ON THE SIDE,

FOLLOWED BY FRESH PICARONES **THAT TU MADRE** COOKED AND HOOKED UP WITH PRIDE

BROWN-BLACK, LIKE BUFFALO STEW AND
BANGIN' **MEMPHIS BBQ**
OXTAILS, CALI FISH TACOS, **CATFISH**, **SHRIMP & GRITS**, LOCO MOCO, MANDI, **LOUISIANA ROUX**
GUMBO BROWN, LIKE SANCOCHO, PURLOO,
OR SOME HEARTY **OKRA SOUP**
TAPADO AND **RASTA PASTA BROWN**,
THAT'LL MAKE YOU SLAP **YO MOMMA**,
THEN **WAKE UP** AND APOLOGIZE,
FO' SHE GIVE YO **A$$** THE **BOOT**

I GOT THAT ***PURPLE*** *BLACK*, Y'ALL!
LIKE PURPLE RICE IN GHANA, **THAILAND**,
AND KOREA, THAT'LL KEEP YOU **WARM** IN THE **FALL**
ALOO BAINGAN BLACK, WITH **PURPLE EGGPLANT**, THAT COULD FEED A WHOLE PARTY **HALL**
THAT **SOUTH AFRICAN PURPLE SWEET** POTATO **BLACK**, THAT'LL MAKE YOU GIVE YOUR GREAT-GREAT-***GREAT***
GRANDMOTHER A CALL

I SAID CORNED BEEF AND **PURPLE CABBAGE** BLACK, **SO GOOD**, IT'LL TURN YOU INTO MJ, AND MAKE YOU **CLIMB YO** BLACK A$$ *OFF THE WALL*

MY BLACK IS **COLORFUL**!

MY BLACK IS VIBRANT, MY BLACK IS **SWEET**

MY BLACK IS **SAVORY**, MY BLACK IS **FLAVORFUL**

MY BLACK IS **AUTHENTIC**, MY BLACK IS **HEAT**

MY BLACK IS **STRAIGHT-UP**, **IN-YOUR-FACE**, AND **LOUD**

BUT EVEN WHEN IT'S **MIXED-UP**, **SUBTLE** AND **DISCREET**,

MY BLACK IS *ALWAYS* **PROUD**!

Earth, Wind & Heaven

I used to fear death

Until … I died …

Over, and over, and over again

Life's currents swept me in the water,

and pulled me to the deep end

And just when I thought I'd drown in my worries,

God grew me a fin

I opened my fish eyes and saw that,

suddenly, I could swim

Then I got hooked on a landline

And felt my water wings grow into a limb

And just when I walked my way into another heaven,

hell held me down, unleashed its dirty demons,

and unfurled my skin

As soon as my soul sank and smelled the
funk of the devil's den,
I heard feathers hatching, and flapping in endless wind

I've died a million times

Maybe even more

But each time I came back, I was standing closer to
heaven's door

(Red Eye)

As pain pooled in my eyes

I realized why, the **Earth** cries

Raining down on herself, and washing away her worries

Through oceans, lakes, and rivers

So the next time she feels used up and dry

She'll have plenty placenta to pull from, endless milk to deliver

To replenish herself

To feed her own **soul**

Cause if she held all that bubbling nectar inside

Flowers wouldn't **bloom**

Bumblebees would have no resting place

Doves, no treetops to lull passersby

So, I sat. Cleansing. Releasing.

Purifying my path and sanctifying my spirit

And, suddenly, **mountains** moved in my mind

Spiraling streams made way for bountiful valleys

And all it took was a waterway to clear it

Now, when it rains, I smile

The **Earth** and I have something in common

Forever watering seeds.

Eternally flowing.

FREE.

It's Missing Something

It's missing something ...

Throw some pepper on that bih
Put some mo' salt on that ho
It ain't hittin' how I want it
I need that punch that make my jaw hit tha flo'

It needs some onions and some garlic
A couple onomatopoeias will do
Don't call me no alcoholic, but I'm bouta hit it wit' dat
WHOP-DI-WHOP! OOH-WEE-OOH!

Go 'head, pour dat Jack-in-the-box
And let that mothaf%$@ stew
Now sip on *that* metaphor
Call it the "Analogy Brew"

Aaah!

It’s *still* missing something …

Sprinkle in some herbs and some flowers

Maybe some **red** and some **blue**

Hold on, that sh*t a lil’ sour

Gone on ‘head and squeeze some honey in there too

Please, open up and taste it

I think it’s telling a story

Oh, “It’s perfect,” you say

But I think it’s *still* missing something

Now go home and marinate on *that* allegory

PART II

The Buds

THE FAMILY SECRET

I INHERITED YOUR CURSES
THEY FOLLOW ME, THREATENING MY EVERY STEP
FUNNY HOW I WAS BORN IN A CITY NAMED
AFTER EDISON, BUT DON'T PACK A LIGHT BRIGHT
ENOUGH TO CLEAR YOUR DEBTS

MY GRANDADDY WENT BLIND
HE SHOWED ME ALL THE OTHER WAYS HE WAS
BLESSED TO SEE
TOO BAD HIS TWISTED WIRES AND ANTI-
RADIATION TOWERS AIN'T STRONG ENOUGH TO
KEEP YOUR DEMONS OFF ME

THEY LIKE TO GANG UP ON ME
YOU KNOW, BEND THEIR FINGERS UP IN
ALL KINDS OF DEADLY DESIGNS
MY GRANDMOMMA USED TO SLAVE IN A BRICK
CITY FACTORY
BUT I GUESS MY PEACE OF MIND WASN'T PART OF
NAN ONE OF HER DESIGNS

FAMILY TREE FILLED WITH VICTIMS OF PTSD
UNCLES USED TO GET DRUNK, BREAK HOMES,
AND CUT THE FOOL
PROBABLY WHY COUSINS AND NIECES STAGGER-
STEP THEIR WAY TO *BABY DADDIES* WHO LIP-
LOCK WRAY & NEPHEW TO PACIFY THEIR JAZZ,
FUNK, AND BLUES

I TRIED TO CHARLESTON SHAKE 'EM OFF WE
I LINDY-HOPPED TO LOSE THE CIRCLE, TRIED TO
SHIMMY OUR WAY *AWAY* FROM THE CYCLE

HOW DARE I THINK I COULD CAKE WALK MY
CLAN TO SOMETHING DIFFERENT?
KNOWING DAMN WELL THOSE BLOODSUCKERS
WOULD MAKE OUR BABIES HURT TOO,
YOU KNOW THEY *ALWAYS* BEEN LOWDOWN
AND SPITEFUL

BUT I GOT A SECRET THEY CAN'T SEE
GUESS I'LL JUST KEEP THAT PANDORA IN ITS BOX
DIG, THERE'S A MAGIC BREWING IN THE DEPTHS
OF MY SOUL
AND THEY SURE AS HELL AIN'T GOT THE KEY TO
THAT LOCK

SO EYE LET THEM FOLLOW ME, FOLLOW WE,
FOLLOW WE
TO THE POINT OF NO RETURN
'CAUSE THOSE WICKED WITCHES FOUND THE
RIGHT ONE WHEN THEY LATCHED ONTO ME
AND I SPEAK FOR THE WHOLE FAMILY
WHEN I SAY: THEY GONE LEARN!

YIN X YANG

One by one
You kiss my insecurities undone
They melt away from the heat of your fiery signals,
loud, yet tender
Falling to your feet, they bow down in defeat, as they speak,
"I surrender. She is everything."

And I am set free. Finally.
No longer am I haunted by their lies
Constantly echoing in the halls of my mind
I fought, I'd fight
Snatching them from the shadows
Exposing them with my light

I'd always known the truth, but I was getting tired
Then you showed up
David-ing all my Goliaths

It had been a while since you came around

We hadn't touched tongues in a minute

But I'm glad we spoke

I thought I'd lost you, but I found

That seeds buried deep never forget who watered them

when they yearned for infinite growth

Make Me Feel Special

I want you to tell me that I'm beautiful
Like a pretty blue ocean view
That puts **sparkles** in your **eyes**
Or those fancy bright lights way up, that decorate the nighttime skies

Make me feel needed, like the oxygen that you breathe
Or that cool-you-down-when-you-heat-stroke-hot summertime breeze

Show me that I light your fire
Like sun on **Black skin** in the deep, deep South
Or the taste of my sweetness when I press my strawberry lips to your always-anticipating, **blissful-blueberry** mouth

Incite my ears to **peak** when I hear how much you love my scent

Like fields filled with lavender and lilies

Or a garden full of fresh peppermint

I just want to know that I touch your **spirit** in every possible way

Make me feel **special**, sugar, I don't mean to sound cliché

But give me that "ain't-no-woman-even-*close*-to-me" feeling

Every minute, of every hour, every single day

Make me feel special.

THE LIBERATION LETTER

To Whom It May Concern,

When my fears get too loud:

I tie my thoughts up to a string, and balloon them to a cloud
Then watch them drift away in bliss and float over the crowd
That tried to convince me to run away and cower, and
"pipe down" on the proud

When my fears get too bold ...

I wrap my spirit up in the sun, and feel the warmth blanket
me from the cold
And then memories of the courageousness of
my ancestors proceed to unfold
FORWARD! I am reminded
REMEMBER! I am told

I AM STRONG

I AM POWERFUL

I AM FEARLESS

I AM FREE

Ain't no *way* I'ma let no *fears* get the best of me!

I don't believe them

I refuse to submit

I got a mission to complete

A burning fire that will NOT relent

Freedom.

To free my dome.

Unchain my domain. Bring peace to my home.

So put a sock in it fear

You ain't all that brave

I'm choosing to win this war

'Cause I *damn sure* ain't your slave!

Now hear *me* get loud

Fall back and watch *me* get bold

I AM EVERY SINGLE GOOD THING

you insisted I am not, bottled up, waiting to EXPLODE!

BEAUTIFUL

CAPABLE

WORTHY

KIND

So now that you know EXACTLY who I am, kindly pack up all

your bags, and exit out my mind

Signed,

Cecily M. Hillman

Cecily Michelle Hillman

Those Eyes, Mama

Your eyes still shine, Mama

Despite the darkness you've endured

You haven't lost your **sparkle**

In fact, you beam **brighter**

Because you've faced ugliness

Stared it down with those **bright eyes**

And reminded it that you are bigger. Better. Stronger. Softer.

The whole world could fall apart, today or tomorrow

The stars could fall from the sky, the moon could follow

But because of the **light in those eyes**, Mama,

I'll never get lost in sorrow

My faith is BIG because of you and those eyes, Mama

They still shine

I'll never not trust the light in those eyes, Mama

Because **your eyes sparkle like mine**

A Friendly Reminder

If ever you are in doubt, here's a reminder that I'm
forever your friend
When your heart feels heavy, fold your body into my
sanctuary, and let my gospel stir your soul to mend

When flimsy "friends" turn foes
When joy and glory turn to woe
When what was once "yes" turns to hellish hurt
and nasty "no's"
My **spirit** will wrap around every single wound you wear,
like a billion brilliant bows

If the whole world spits fire at your feet,
and threatens you with a drought
Seek refuge in my sea, and **our love** will drown them out

I'll live inside you, forever

And you, inside of me

So never doubt our friendship

Even when the funk, frost, and fog make **US** hard to see

LOVE LIGHTS THE WAY

You're the reason my heart feels light
So I picked up my pen to let our love shine through
The affection we share beams so bright
It burns bulbs that blares the way for brothers
baffled in black, and bewildered in blue

Nuestro amor es GRANDE
So big that it can't fit into words
Love large like the ego of Brother Kanye
But humble enough to protect, listen, and serve

It's softly lulling to you
Tugging at my core
Reminding us to trust that this connection is true
Even when our signals are interrupted by the chaos outside,
twisted up in *their* war

I'll always come back home

That little, mighty fire will surely lead the way
These God-given antennas constantly carry me
to the throne
Where our love will undoubtedly and forever, stay

I Love You...

I love you because I feel safe with you. I love you because your spirit feels good to me—it touches the depths of me, parts that only special souls have keys to unlock.

I love you because your voice comforts me; the sound of your tone makes me forget all my worries, even when unsure lips utter otherwise.

Heart always knows.

I could go on and on and on, but know that I love you because you feel like home.

Love's Synonyms

I love you like a thousand **kisses planted** on your body,
one by one
I **taste** you like a million wishes to forever have your
sweetness sugarcoat my tongue

I **praise** you like the sun caressing my **third eye** on a warm
summer day
I **crave you** like the moonlight **undressing** your
body, and mine, in the **nighttime** as we lay

I **save** you like **saints and sinners** swimming for
repentance in sanctified rivers
I **feel** you like that **tender embrace** that touches
you in the right place, and makes your **body quiver**

I **comfort** you like a cool breeze
when you're **hot** in-between your knees

I **seduce** you like a **butterfly sings to a sunflower**
Or a hummingbird **serenades** her oak trees

I dig you, daddy, just like the Earth
I **nurture** you like you were groomed in my **womb**
and I gave you **bearth**

I love you like I've never loved you before
That just means **my love for you is only beginning**,
and I have **forever** to love you, plus **forever more**

Ancient Addiction

You poured your honey all over me
Now I'm sweet, just like you

I wish that I could tell you how much I miss you
For now, this jar of my molasses will do

Put it on your windowsill, let it bathe in the sun
So when you dip your fingers in it, and just before you put it
on your salivating tongue ...

Your two lips will warn your 6 senses of this
ancient addiction
And then, you'll remember that I'm the *ONE*

I'M IN LOVE WITH YOU...

Can't you tell???

With those lips ... those eyes ...
Every Hershey-flavored kiss
You put me under your spell

Now I'm *looooooooooooooooveeee* sick
And I don't want to get well
I'll prance with you at the peaks of heaven
And protect you through the pits of hell

I'm always by your side, God
Watching you, pushing you to prevail
I'll be your **guiding light**,
helping you see through the darkness of the veil

And when worry makes you want to wrinkle up
and wane into a shell
I'll be there waiting to remind you of who you are,
filling you up with love, until all your fears are quelled

I'm in love with you ...

And it will NEVER stop
So though your journey's been tough
Know that I'm climbing this mountain with you,
conquering this rock

And as we march steady, just like the tick of the clock
Know that one day soon, the struggle will be over
And our love will be planted at the top

Holy Matrimony

You ever been kissed by the ocean?
Seduced by her waves?
Or are you afraid of her motion?
Petrified to take a sip of the potion that your body craves?

Are you intrigued by her ebb and flow?
Do her liquid limbs take a piece of you each time
they come and go?
Or do you keep your feet planted on the pavement
so the depth of her divinity you'll never know?

Are you intrigued by the stars when you look up at the sky?
Does the darkness illuminate your outer starkness
and make you wonder "why"?

Do you see that same magic when you look me in the eye?
And does the possibility of finding all your answers
make you turn away and accept the lie?

Can you feel all of eternity when you swim in my
deep pool of passion?
And do all the treasures you find make you want to
bottle up, this sweet, sugary stuff, and experience me
in only a fraction?

Because ...

You see, BAY-BEE:
Just like the sky, and same as the sea
I hold the power of the ENTIRE universe inside of me
I spark all the pigments of your imagination with
my electricity
Maybe that's the reason your being craves me in more ways
than just sexually

You feel me in your spine, in the corners of your mind
I touch you in ways that far exceed humanly perception of
space, distance, and time
We're forever intertwined, connected by the Divine
You live *inside* of me,

so there’s never a need to question if you are “mine”

You ever been kissed by the ocean?
Seduced by her waves?
And did all her sacred jewels lather you like lotion?
And help you slip through the confines of this Earthly maze?
Did she wash away all the fiery sins that
threatened to set your soul ablaze?
And did the power of her gentle lovin’ break away the
shackles that once made you a slave?

You ever recognize the light shining from the stars
when you look up at the sky?
Do they remind you of the sparkles that ignite the
everlasting pathways between you and eye?
And do you realize that we will ALWAYS have a forever tie?
Together, twisting and turning, wallowing in the lows, and
lifted on the high
Until our flesh feeds the ocean, and our souls sail away
in the sky

The Butterfly Effect

I've spent eons earning my wings.
Hurting.
Toiling.
Making mistakes.
Learning.
Shedding old ways that no longer served.

Now that my caterpillar legs have kicked their way to kites,
watch me soar.
Sprinkling my magic in every dark place that I once endured

Growth is hard.
But stagnation is harder.

I choose. To grow.
Unfolding ...

I'M UP HIGH, POPPA

Can you see me?
I'm way up high, Poppa
I'm making music on the clouds, tap dancing in the sky, Poppa

You promised you'd be my safety net,
if I ever needed to fall
But it's looking like you done pumped me up so good, Poppa
I ain't 'fraid to drop at all

Thanks to your guts and your grip,
I let loose and trusted my wings
Hey, Poppa, I know you see me twirling 'round in the heavens, doing all kinds of whimsy things

I'll come back down soon enough, and I know you'll be right there waiting
But I sure ain't in no rush, Poppa
'Cause the air up here is fresh, free, and *umm, umm, umm!* Intoxicating!

I'm way up high, Poppa
Yes, it feels outstanding
And I promise to make you proud, Poppa
With a marathon-timed, Simone Biles-styled, Olympic Gold landing

I Just Wanna Dance

I want to dance
Like my ancestors are speaking through my limbs
Let them Rumba through my hips
And Rock & *Roooollllllll* their remedies
Up and down my spine, activating each vertebrae
Releasing wild rhythms like a xylophone in motion

I need my feet to sign their freedom in Samba
SHINE, SHOES! SHINE!
As we Afrobeat up and down the street
Shimmering and shaking, sizzling Salsa,
Cooking up rebellious heat

PLEASE BELLY, DANCE!
Like you've got Baladi vibrating in your pants
Wine pon di walls, beck and call
Sweat out my ponytail as we slither and snake
Around your dancehall

BOUNCE, BOOTY! BOUNCE!

Like you've got banjos bumping in your backseat

Jookin' with some jazzy Gospel to announce

Or funky goombay drums Kompa-calling, Soca-and-Spouge spelling

With carnival commands to pronounce

I just want to Hula and Hoop Dance

Clap my hands in Cumbia

And feel my fingers flutter,

Fancy and fierce, like I'm emancipating a kalimba

SPEAK, BODY!

You've got some hips and hops,

Some Neo Soul, and Rhythm & Blues to unleash

Let's burn down the house, light up the disco,

Torch down the club

Then watch our crazy legs Merengue twist all the way to

Some Techno love

Break those bonds with your karate kicks, capoeira fly
Chop away the chains with silat, Kung Fu kiss the sky
Plant your toes in Taekwondo to conjure up all
Earth's sacred memories
Purify your temple with some good old-fashioned
Muay Thai

And then...
Let your arms Amapiano, your neck Eskista, and your
'Bows Benga
Because your ancestors are speaking. And they say,
"You are free."

Body.

Don't you remember?

PART III

The Roses

¡Mama's Home!

I think Momma's waking up
She's coming back to us

But really, it's a matter of remembering

Once she remembers everything, she will remember
that she *IS* everything

And *EVERYTHING* that's been pollutin' everything
that her womb has birthed, nurtured and nursed ...

Hmph. #Barbaric

Dad's Bouquet

Your prudence has paved paths unshakable
Your protection has provided the courage I need to pace
with grace, and remember I am unbreakable

Your presence has always been felt in spirit,
this much is true
I'm eternally grateful for your guidance,
so here is my gift to you:

A special bouquet to ease your aches,
like the sweetness of your favorite wine
Savor these notes and let the flavors butterfly beautiful
memories, just like grapes on a vine

Don't forget the chocolates, they compliment the
experience, like classic art
Same as the love I have for my dad, that gets greater with
time, and will forever decorate my heart

Life's Blooms

Find joy in the small things ...

Like watching a flower bloom
Beauty blossoming from the confines of a cocoon

Analogies. Reminders.
Gentle guides wiping the fog from our blinders:

Life if filled with sorrow and woe
Pain is inevitable, of this we know
But it is in the darkest of spaces that we find our wands
And unleash the magic that helps us grow

BLACK HAIR

Bangs bantu'd, bantu'd bangs

Butterfly braids, baby hairs: *LAID!*

Barber sharp blades box out high top fades, beards bloomed, groomed and shaved

Beads bejeweled, berets go: *BLANG!*

Big ole heads combed *HOT!* Burned, balmed, and finger-waved

Locs liberated, liberating locks

Lined up, links parted, growing like lifetime stocks

Aht! Aht! Aht! Ain't nan anaconda head

Aiming Amazon agua, summer poolside

Assaulting this wavy weave ... or

Crinkled curls come out of caps

Crimped up and calling cousins to crush culprits

Crowned with Caesar cuts and coils carved up like colossal coliseums

Kinked up knots, kneaded up top, on heads that's tender

Knitted like knacks only kinfolk, kings, and Kemetic queens remember

Hallelu*jah*! Hair so heavenly
Heathens hail its history from here to
Hong Kong, 7 days a week, January through December

Ancient antennas activated
Afro arms arch like ankhs and arrows stretched to
Aten (Ah-ton)

I*t's missing something!* Just
Itch that scratch in yo scalp to unlock
Interlaced memories forgotten

Relax, and recollect **ropes of regality** hanging from
Royal rooms, waiting ... on
Rolled up wraps to **roll out railroads** that
Recall the **roots** in their **routes**, and the **power** in their **stations**

#BlackQueens

When we unlearn the lies that we've been told
We'll realize our value is greater than gold
When we accept the kinks in our hair
We will see the beauty that is there

When we turn the pain into gain
And wield the wounds from
traumas meant to make us insane
We will re-ascend to our thrones
Born from the royal seeds that were long ago sown

Little Black girl: DO YOU KNOW WHO YOU ARE!?

Rhythm in your hips
Plump like a bumblebee stung your honey lips
The WORLD is guided by your star
Melanin drippin', ass sittin', head pattin'
when yo' scalp is itchin'

ERRRRRRRR-BODY wanna know the

recipes in ***yo'* kitchen**!

Just tell them **watch** and **pay attention**

But we all **know** they ***BEEN*** **lookin'**, they ***BEEN*** **listenin'**

These days everybody's **braided** up, twerkin' with

Sarah Baartman **butts**, and bronze **skin** **glistenin'**

But don't take it from **me**

Just look **around** and **you'll** **see**, **exactly** what I **mean**

We are the originators

The creators

Mother's to the **universe**

#BlackQueens

A Love Divine

To reap it, you gotta sow it
Plant your seeds in my soil
I'll be bearing fresh fruits
before you know it

But first, you gotta ...

Water me with your affection
Shower me with time
Shield me with protection
Pluck the weeds from my vine
Nourish me with your light
Feed my soul with your sun
The light in you beckons my branches
I willingly cum

Baby, boo, this is more than physical
This love is divine
With it, patience and faith
have grown aroused
Because our 6 senses it tastes
better with time

It's been decades ...
years, months, weeks
Now our tree of life is ripe with goods, seducing you
to part your lips and eat
It took a lifetime for this lifeline to penetrate the Earth
and kiss the sky
Seasons spring lessons,
tenderly warming winter from our hearts
While forcing lethal leaves to
fall and die

A love this heavenly took some time,
but it sure is sweet

Tantalizing to the flesh, satisfying
to the mind
But beneath the surface,
the roots run deep

A love divine.

DEJÁ TWO

My spirit recognized you
Even before words reached out to embrace
I looked into your eyes and I knew

I told you last lifetime that I'll forever find you

And.

You'll always find me. Too.

Those Eyes…

They ignited an inferno in my soul. I felt it deep down in my belly. I tried to douse the fire, but I couldn't run from the flames.

There was no denying it.

I knew you were the one.

Us. 4ever.

Fear: are you stuck in the illusion?

Can you hear the voice of God? Or are you distracted by

all the confusion?

Have you mastered your mind, or are your fences weak

and defenseless from the intrusions?

Do you trust the truth? Or are you more satisfied with

the delusions?

I hear you talking Lord, but can you speak up?

This ain't no easy marathon, I've been *dying* to keep up

Soon as your whispers get louder and louder,

that raggedy doubt starts to creep up

I want to get close to you, and meet you at the peak,

but ...

You're afraid

I've gifted you with the blueprint, but you don't believe in the

magic from which you were made
Did you think that I didn't hear your heart when you got down on your knees and prayed?
I said I would never forsake you, so even when you tripped and stumbled, I carried you through the maze

WE ALL KNOW WHAT'S REAL: OUR MIND MAY FORGET, BUT HEART AND BODY REMEMBER
THEY KEEP US ON THE PATH, EVEN WHEN HEAD HAS ITS OWN AGENDA
WHEN BRAIN BREAKS AWAY AND BECOMES A SELF-PROCLAIMED CONTENDER
LISTEN TO THAT LITTLE FIRE INSIDE AND ...
SURRENDER

Pack Light

That suitcase weighs a ton

Backpack filled with bricks

Gotta pack a little lighter, son

Before you book that flight, then miss

The Wild Release

The rain's tap dancing on my window again.

Mother Earth must've heard my body aching for a **wild**

release.

So she cried for me.

4 Rebel

My cup could never be more full, or so I thought ...
until I laid eyes on you

The first time I held you in my arms and you drank from my
breast, that little pump that we call a heart, exploded
Like a trillion pieces of confetti
Painting love all over me

And then you looked into my eyes
And I saw every single *good* thing
that the Lord has ever made:

Oceans, seas, the stars & sky
I saw the strength of every ancestor
The quiet power of our planet
I saw little me. I saw *you*.

My eyes never shined so bright

The spark in yours ignited the light in mine

In love, I am

As you grow,
my heart expands with you
I never knew I could be so full
But here I am, overflowing

Your little feet
Those tiny hands
Every. Single. Time. You touch me.
Oh, what a beautiful feeling

In love, I am

Your smile dismantles wayward walls that
long ago took root in my heart
I find myself crafting cute ways to make you laugh
So that my heart can continue to run rivers

And rinse away those walls
Sprouting flowers in their place instead

My garden is full

In love, I am

Now, whenever I feel dry
I cuddle up next to your little body
And soak up your endless love

Fill me up, baby
Your mommy is overflowing

Because of YOU

And you have a BIG cup to sip from, *forever*

In love, we are

Basquiat's Baby

(To ▽Chin)

When you touch me
Old wounds are healed
There's a magic in your hands
Some good juju in your energy field

Your fingertips trace bibles on my body
I bathe in every scripture
Without a single word spoken
Your 10 points orate the perfect picture

My Basquiat Baby

Even if I were blind
I would still be able to see
All this colorful love your palms pour over me

Painting Polaroids of memories from
lives lived before
Yes, I remember every moment as your gentle bristles
mend, illuminate and explore

I want more

I could never get enough ...

Of your healing hands
Your therapeutic touch

The Love Cycle

When I'm wrapped up in your arms
My pump fills up
And waterfalls cascade all over my body
I'm tingling, baby

Come take a sip from this love cup
And feel me
Fill YOU up
And erupt wild waterways all over *you*

We could feed a whole jungle with our
river runs
The Earth will never go dry
I'm so filled up with your hurricane love that
at times, these floods force me to cry

Yes, your torrents and tides are washing
over me again
So I wind up right back in your arms, giving
you tsunamis
And getting my pump filled up
All the way up

And it feels like we'll do this ...
Again ... and again ... and again
Because, my sweet water baby, with us,
there is no beginning

We have no end

Pain's Exhibition

What am I supposed to do with all this pain?
It's way too wide to pack away in my suitcase and
send sailing on a train
Way too turbulent to tie down and
fly away on a fancy freedom plane
And too damn resistant to strap up to my pickup truck, and
send coasting on heaven's highway, straight down liberty lane

It's too *ugly* to fold up pretty and nice, and hide in my closet
Way too *filthy* to rinse clean and declare itself redeemed under
my faucet

Wish I could snip it, clip it, nip it, rip it
Tear it into tiny pieces, stuff it in a doomed duffle bag, and zip it
That way, I won't hear it when it yells and screams
Hollerin' 'bout how it's *way too MEAN* for me to *ever* escape its
nasty little fangs and clings

I really want to stomp it out
Push it way down, I mean WAY down, into the pavement
Make it feel my wrath for all the years I stayed stuck in a cage,
melting in mental enslavement

How 'bout I'll just make it burn?
For all the hell it erupted in the pit of my belly, I'll feed it to the
flames and watch it wither, squeal and squirm
Yeah, watch it cry out, stop, drop, and turn
Make it roast and toast real slow, like the sting of a perm
So next time that *BIG* rack wants to come back to attack,
it'll think twice
Yeah, that's the way it'll learn

Better yet, I'll gift it to somebody else
Maybe then I could finally feel free
Wrap these wounds up real tight
And plant the package under my lover's Xmas tree

He'll open it up and chop it down like wood
Let it all disintegrate and fertilize the Earth, just like a righteous

healer should
And maybe Mother Nature would transform my madness into
something beautiful, art to uplift the greater good

If you happen to be
Reading this soliloquy
That means I unearthed the answer to this lifelong debate
I took the weight of my woes and wielded it into something
monumental, a documented lesson to demonstrate
The pain? You'll *never* obliterate
Embrace the aches, turn them to paint,
and decorate the darkest details of your fate

Now you have a classic,
a masterpiece to which people can relate
So hang it on your trophy wall and take it all in ...
Breathe ... grieve ... meditate
Revel at your framed pain and all the sullied strokes that
make it great
Then call upon the MOST HIGH to invite the right souls to your
pain's exhibition, and watch your work: EMANCIPATE

Roots & Roses

About the Author

Cecily Michelle Hillman is a Newark, New Jersey native who started her professional writing career as an intern at BET Networks when she was 21-years-old. She went on to lend her voice to major media platforms such as Ebony, Madame Noire, and For Harriet. In 2015, Cecily kickstarted her own entertainment hub, Miss Cm (formally addressed as MissCM.com, now MissCM.org), where she mixed her love for journalism with her passions for blogging, educating people on, and learning about, the African diaspora, and celebrating Black culture.

Miss CM has since been embraced for it's unicorn approach to journalism and blogging, reaching hundreds of thousands of readers in every corner of the planet. In 2017, the seasoned writer released her debut novel, *Accepted*, which is globally heralded as a literary chef-d'oeuvre.

Cecily Michelle earned an AA in Liberal Arts from Essex County College, a BA in Music from Ramapo College of NJ, and is a 2009 graduate of Rutgers New Brunswick's Center for American Women and Politics (CAWP) program. Cecily is a former teacher at North Star CMS and KIPP LIFE, and holds a partial MAT from Relay Newark. The multi-hyphenate creative is also founder and CEO of the wholistic health and beauty brand CM's Naturals.

You can learn more about Cecily and her various initiatives at misscm.org.

Made in the USA
Coppell, TX
30 June 2026

83614014R00056